# WITHIN
# THE TEMPLE
# OF ISIS

# MORE WILDSIDE CLASSICS

*Please see www.wildsidepress.com for a complete list!*

# WITHIN THE TEMPLE OF ISIS

## BELLE M. WAGNER

**WILDSIDE PRESS**

# WITHIN THE TEMPLE OF ISIS

This edition published 2005 by Wildside Press, LLC.
www.wildsidepress.com

# TO MY HUSBAND,

Henry Wagner, M.D.,
IN ACKNOWLEDGEMENT OF HIS TRUE WORTH AS A
WARRIOR
IN THE CAUSE OF TRUTH, AND HIS DEVOTION TO THE
BROTHERHOOD AND SISTERHOOD OF MAN, AND THE
FATHERHOOD AND MOTHERHOOD OF GOD, I
DEDICATE THIS BOOK.
BY THE AUTHORESS.

# PUBLISHER'S PREFACE.

We are safe in saying that "Within The Temple of Isis" is unique and stands alone. There is no other book in print like it, and if Solomon of old had not said, "There is nothing new under the sun," we would be inclined to contradict him.

"Within the Temple of Isis" God's word was law as interpreted by his Hierophants; their oneness with the fountain of Being made them conscious of Nature's secret operations, and enabled them, as it does the wise ones of today, to enter the Temple of Isis and observe the hidden mysteries concealed behind the veil.

Purity of motive and sincerity of purpose brought its own reward to them of old as it does to those of today who purify themselves before seeking for the knowledge and wisdom hidden within the "Holy of Holies" — "The Temple of Isis."

Isis means Mother of all, while Osiris means Father of all.

The Temple of Two Truths as matter and spirit must be realized within.

The Polar Opposites are those of sex dually expressed as two poles of one law or principle as taught by Hermetic Philosophy before the law of polarization of spirit into matter, and matter back into spirit, can be understood.

The Alchemist and the Astrologer, alike, possess this wisdom, and it was this knowledge that made the Priests Kings of Egypt, so justly famous as Magicians or Wise Men.

They still exist in spirit realms and can transmit to this plane of earth their wisdom, that would make earth a veritable paradise if only the race could be made to realize its magical powers.

Scientific inventions of great moment to the race are thus projected to the earth, and spiritual Adepts in occult laws will again revive the "Wisdom Religion" upon earth in all its beauty and grandeur as the western race becomes fitted intellectually and spiritually to receive it.

Nature ever repeats herself in cycles of time on the spiritual and mental, as well as the physical planes of life.

End, there is none. Time and eternity are the ever-present Now, so far as the spirit is concerned. Therefore, the readers of this strange occult book will some day realize its truths as realities of natural law on the spiritual planes of life. It is a clear, practical statement of Soul Marriage and of Soul Transfer from one earthly temple to that of another.

Nature's laws are ever the same; therefore, the same experiences herein narrated are applicable to Neophytes seeking soul initiation today as they were in the days of The Temple of Isis, and if the veil of Isis could be raised for one single moment the world would be startled by the mysterious revelations disclosed.

To the Seers and the Occult Initiates alike, this book will appeal with magical force. Its truths are those of the soul and spirit, and can await the reader's soul development for verification.

Truth needs no apology; therefore, none will be offered as an excuse for this publication. It is our desire that our readers may some day know for themselves that Truth is indeed stranger than Fiction.

# INTRODUCTION.

In presenting this little volume to our readers we ask them to accept it, not as fiction, but as divine truth as to the laws herein revealed.

Not a statement is made that is not possible to the divine will of man. Although it can not be proven to your outward knowledge, do not reject and declare it is not true.

History will teach you there actually existed a "Temple of Isis," and the translations thereof, although many of them are very incorrect, of the wonderful magic therein performed, lead one to think there was some Wisdom issued from that Temple that is yet beyond the human family, as a whole, to understand.

"The Temple of Isis" exists no more in external form, and the Hierophants of that Temple have passed from this to the spiritual planes above. But, need we think by that, the blind forces of Nature can no more be controlled? The forces are just the same today, but man's mind fails to grasp the truth that history repeats itself.

Mighty Hierophants are upon the earth today, in embryo, and when the time comes that points favorably for active spiritual work on the Western Continent, they will be called forth and Egypt will not be ashamed of her true children nor their works.

The Wisdom Religion of Egypt still exists and we can contact that Wisdom by the development of our souls. Even do the Wise Men of the East, that was, exert their spiritual influence upon us today if we but knew it.

The trouble lies with us not with them. They will never conceal it from the honest soul truly seeking for Light, Life and Love.

Follow us carefully to the end, without prejudice, and when you have finished, if you still think it fiction, strive to prove its falsity and stop not until you have reached that stage of soul unfoldment that will enable you to occupy that plane whereby you can stand beside the great Hierophants of "The Temple of Isis."

THE AUTHORESS.

# WITHIN THE TEMPLE OF ISIS.

# CHAPTER I.

## THE REVELATION OF THE ASTROLOGER.

Although the hour was very late, near midnight, the Priestess had just retired to her apartments for repose.

The Rites of the day had been extremely long and fatiguing, as they always were for a Priestess of Isis attendant upon the burial service of one in high rank; and a great nobleman of the land, as well as a near relative of the Priestess herself, had been buried that day.

Thus personal sorrow had mingled with and added weight to the impressive and solemn grandeur of the occasion, yet, strangely enough her mind was neither with the events of the day nor the dead, but her thoughts were resting now where they had wandered many times throughout the day, namely, to her little handmaid and special attendant, as well as Vestal in the Temple, Sarthia.

Sarthia, who at the very beginning of the Chants and Litany, had failed in her part and had, with such a pitiable moan and beseeching glance at her, been hastily withdrawn from the assembly and assisted to the private courts.

Poor child, she thought, the strain upon her emotions, the solemn occasion, was too great for her in view of the crisis, which all unknown to her, must be now impending. However, upon learning from an attendant that the young girl was resting quietly and apparently not ill, she had not herself personally visited her, but concluded to wait until morning.

Once, twice, thrice, just as the Priestess had, as it were, passed the border-land of sleep the pale face, with its pleading eyes and plaintive cry, had started her back to vivid consciousness.

"Ah! this will never do," she said, springing to her feet. "Something is indeed wrong," and taking up her mantle she glided swiftly through the corridors, and a few moments later was bending over the silent and motionless form of Sarthia.

Noiseless as had been the approach of the Priestess some interior vibration had informed Sarthia of her coming and, with a quivering and swift movement, she sprang from her couch and threw herself impulsively into the arms of the Priestess.

"Ah! sweet Mother, well beloved of our blessed and divine Isis, hear me and help me," said the girl, in a whisper, tense and low, so low as only to reach the listening ear of the Priestess.

"Speak child," answered the Priestess, caressingly clasping Sarthia to her bosom with one strong arm, and with the other making soft, mesmeric passes over her trembling body.

"Ah! thank you, sweet Mother; this is so good and kind of you to come to me tonight. I have suffered so all day from your thought; you have been disappointed in your Sarthia and with reason, too. A Vestal, who all but faints at the sight of death, is not made of the stuff required in the Temple Service. But, believe me, dear

Priestess, the trouble is far deeper than appears upon the surface. The Ritual this morning but furnished the occasion or, rather, hastened some crisis that was already near at hand. For some time now I am haunted by most potent premonitions of a violent death. Night after night, dark apparitions hang around my bed, and only last night I awoke to find the Bird of Nu, the Owl, from out the inner Sanctuary of the Temple, perched upon my pillow and shaking his head and croaking at me most mournfully."

"What!" exclaimed the Priestess. "The Bird of Nu. Ah! this is indeed very serious. The matter must be investigated at once. But, my child, if all these portents prove true, do you fear death? Have all our teachings been in vain? Have you made so little progress in knowledge and the philosophy of existence as to be overcome by dark shadows and grow faint in the presence of the sentiment and show of an external ceremony? The pageantry, which appeals so overwhelmingly to the emotions of the outside world, is the necessary means of teaching the people these awful and stupendous mysteries of life and death. But the Initiate should be sustained by actual experiences within these hidden realms and possess a knowledge of their inner nature which places him on a plane far above the reach of Fear; besides being endowed with that burning love for wisdom which calmly discerns good in evil, and immortal life in the shadow, called death. Do not think I am chiding you, my child. I am only seeking to recall my real Sarthia, who is incapable of Fear, back to this physical expression called body.

"There, already the bright soul shines again with its usual clear light. Hold it firmly and do not let it flicker so again, and now I must leave you to seek an interview with the chief of the Astrologers. The record and Horoscope of your birth must be carefully looked up, and the meaning of these portents determined. Good-night, my child."

With a kiss, fond and maternal, the Priestess withdrew. She proceeded leisurely and thoughtfully toward a distant part of the Temple, having first dispatched a messenger before her to announce her coming, seeking an audience, well knowing that at this now early hour of morning the Astrologer Priests would all be in the midst of their busiest studies, calculations and most profound observations.

But Sarthia, when left alone, although marvelously calmed and comforted by the tender presence and lofty words of her idolized Priestess could not compose herself to sleep. Instead, she soon floated into a state of restful contemplation, drifting from one topic to another, until suddenly she found herself confronted by a most intensely vivid and startling vision. "Can it be?" Yes, true enough, there sat the venerable Astrologer holding in his hand before him, her chart of birth. Beside him, engaged in completing the necessary calculations, sat the scribe and youthful Astrologer Priest, Hermo. There was a strange pallor over his face and a compression of the lips which betrayed unusual emotion. The Priestess was partially facing them, composed, yet with a serious thoughtfulness of mien.

At last, Hermo, looking up, said, "The directions for the present year of life are made out, and the fatal arc carefully computed, Venerated Master," and handed his work to the Astrologer who took it, studied a moment briefly, and turned to the Priestess.

"What is the result, Venerated Father?" she asked gently.

The Astrologer slowly shook his head and replied impressively, "According to all the laws of our Science, and you know how true they are, the physical organism of Sarthia can not survive this present cycle of yonder fair Goddess of the night." And, with a majestic move, he pushed aside a curtain, revealing the Moon now low in the west.

"So short a time," said the Priestess. "Tomorrow night will be the full, and must we indeed lose our Sarthia before another new Moon? What is the nature of these evil influences?"

"The planets, in their configurations, indicate sudden and violent dissolution," was the reply.

"Ah, now," said Sarthia to herself resolutely, at this point turning away from the vision, "now I understand it all," and with a feeling of amaze at her newly-attained clairvoyance she fell into a deep and refreshing sleep.

# CHAPTER II.

## IN THE PRESENCE OF THE HIEROPHANT.

With the first waking moments a sharp pang recalled to Sarthia the vision and its revealments of the previous night. But her mind had fully recovered its philosophic tone and she proceeded about her customary routine of duties, calm and firm, and, as is often the case, in view of some inevitable and stupendous catastrophy close at hand, life only seemed larger, more intensely real. So, when later in the day she received summons to meet the great Hierophant and High Priest, what, at any other time, would have seemed a most momentous event, appeared now only in the light of the expected and necessary.

As she was ushered into the presence of the Holy Father the whole apartment seemed pervaded by an atmosphere of genial warmth and electrical-giving life which somehow emanated from the inner nature of the Priest himself, radiating also spiritual and mental, as well as physical force.

For some moments the Hierophant regarded the

young Vestal in silence, but Sarthia was conscious that he was reading her inmost thought and motive like an open book, even down to her vision of the Astrologer and his fatal announcement regarding her life.

"My child," he said at length, "are you ready for the great change now already at hand?"

"No, Father, not ready but resigned to what seems to be the inevitable decrees of the planets that rule my physical destiny."

"Thou hast well said thou art not ready. Your life has yet but only begun for you. Its experiences, its many lessons and duties, are all unlearnt and you would pass to the spirit world immatured. Your young soul, like fruit plucked from the tree too soon, would ripen slowly, losing many of its flavors and never attaining certain of its best and highest qualities, for as you well know, progress in the next stage of existence depends upon the attainments in this.

"Thou art not ready, yet say you are willing to bow to the inevitable. This is wise, still have you not heard it said many times that man is the arbiter of his own destiny and that the soul was the inheritor of God-like powers by which it could rise to the plane whereby it ruled, instead of obeying the blind or planetary forces of Nature?"

"True, O Venerated Father, I have indeed heard all this, but I am very ignorant. Are there such possibilities for my soul?" and somehow imperceptibly hope began to dawn within her heart and quicken the life forces.

"Ruling the blind forces of Nature is very like ruling the wild beast, although the beast is much stronger than man and capable of tearing him to pieces, yet man, by forethought, can evade or trap and chain or otherwise overcome him. So my child, there are ways wherein man, assisted by his own knowledge, and by the instruction of departed spirits; aye, by the immortal Gods themselves, can evade even the malefic planets in their devastating course.

"To my clairvoyant vision, as I now at this moment look at you, every minute atom of your physical organism is in the subtle process of depolarization from unity toward chaos and disintegration. You are not yourself conscious of this condition only as it has been revealed to you, for your soul is so alive that it has become almost unconscious of its physical expression and for this very reason the shock of dissolution would be all the greater when it did come; for example, witness your unexpected collapse yesterday morning. Ah! sudden death is a most deplorable calamity, and your pitiable state of mind was but a foretaste of what would be the state of your soul for many long years, if you had died then, and will yet be, to a less extent now, unless this swift-coming blow can be evaded.

"However, in case the worst comes to worst, you have about ten days more of this external life and under our special care and preparation you can live years of experience in hours of physical time, and your soul thus equipped may courageously enter upon its journey to the spirit world. Rest assured, my child, everything possible shall be done for you."

"Ah, thank you; thank you, kind and good Father," exclaimed Sarthia, casting herself at the feet of the Hierophant and, with tears streaming from her eyes, kissing the hem of his robe.

"But, truly life is sweet, especially to the young, is it not, my child?" said the Priest, gently raising Sarthia to his side and holding her trembling form in a firm clasp. "Happily, there is an alternative which we have to offer for your most careful consideration and decision.

"Listen now, and give me your closest attention. Know you the young Princess Nu-nah?" Sarthia bowed assent.

"For now these many weeks she lies in a semi-conscious condition, the soul hovering about its earthly temple uncertain whether to go or stay. In some respects her condition corresponds with your own, only that with you, as dissolution approaches, your soul grows brighter and more active, while hers becomes more and more latent; this result being largely the difference of environment — a contrast of the soul unfoldment possible in Temple life and that amid the distractions of the outside world.

"Tonight, the night of the full Moon, the Princess Nu-nah will be brought to the Temple and the Rites performed initiatory to the soul's great change. You, also, my child, must bear her company. The same journey lies before you both and you can go hand in hand through the dark valley of the shadow of death.

"And now, right here is a point where all will depend upon *your* decision. It is possible for us, by aid of the arts of Magic known to us, to bring your two souls in such magnetic rapport that at a certain point the vibrations of the two will, for a single instant of time, be in unison. At that momentous instant the polarity of the two souls can be interchanged so that the subsequent vibrations of your soul will draw you toward Nu-nah's body, while Nu-nah's soul will be drawn toward your organism, and thus will be accomplished the first great step in the drama.

"This great change will hasten the physical crisis in each organism. But your soul, while connected with Nu-nah's body, can easily overcome the malefic planetary influences which would destroy it if she were there; while her soul in your body renders *nil*, by its very non-resistance, the influences which would be absolutely fatal were you still there when the evil descends. And thus do you evade the blind forces of Nature. Two lives are spared for the duties and experiences of this world. This will be the second part of the drama, and now comes the third and last point to consider, the Result.

"In just the proportion as this is a most stupendous change in your soul life, so indeed, perhaps, even appalling to your present comprehension, will be the effect.

"After your soul has once entered its new temple it will be obliged to remain there polarized by the new forces set in operation while passing the crisis. Then, Sarthia, our bright and well-beloved Vestal, will henceforth be known as Princess Nu-nah, and will be obliged for a time to live the life and perform the duties of the Princess.

"On the other hand, the Princess Nu-nah will put on the external body of our Vestal Sarthia and enter upon the life of the Temple Service, but with this difference; that while this change is consciously made by you, Nu-nah will probably never know it until she passes finally to the spirit world. Her past life has already faded from memory while consciousness of the new life will dawn gradually as upon an infant, and therefore, since she can not be consulted in the matter, the decision rests solely with you.

"Tonight, at midnight, your answer will be required. Until then, fare thee well, and God be with you."

# CHAPTER III.

## THE MIDNIGHT OF THE FULL MOON.

It yet lacked several hours of the fateful midnight, as Sarthia, her body perfumed and annointed, according to the prescribed rites, was borne by faithful attendants from the bath into the courts of the Sanctuary and placed upon a couch beside another, upon which already rested the unconscious form of the lovely Princess Nu-nah.

But Sarthia, although to an external, observer as unconscious as the fair Nu-nah, was never more intensely awake, every atom of her being and soul alert to all transpiring about her and conveyed to her through her marvelous new gifts of clairvoyance and clairaudience.

Never, with the external eye, had she seen more vividly the vista upon vista of columns and corridors winding in and about the Sanctuary, now illuminated by the full-orbed Queen of the Night, which she could see shining through a certain archway, and her heart thrilled as she counted the number of archways fair Luna must pass until, at midnight, she would shine down through the one just above her.

Already had begun the weird chants, interspersed with solos of exquisite harmonies of stringed and wind instruments — responses and echoes.

Incense burned and perfumes arose and blended in an indescribable union with melody and motion, while as the fragrant vapors from the burning censers wafted and wreathed about the colonnades and porticoes, Spirit forms added their presence to the sublime scene, bringing with them flowers, aromas and harmonies from the divine abodes of the very Gods themselves.

Oblivious of the passage of time, while intently absorbed in every minutest detail of the wonders passing about her, Sarthia was almost becoming drowsy, when suddenly, the Moon looked in upon her, fast nearing the final archway, and yet she was undecided. She turned and gazed upon her companion, mentally asking, "Can I become Nu-nah?"

Nu-nah was very beautiful and a Princess. But Sarthia was also beautiful and the blood in her veins was royal, though of a different branch from the present ruling House.

Nu-nah was cold and haughty, accustomed to rule and be obeyed.

Sarthia was humble externally, a Vestal of the Temple, but in her mind and soul as imperious as a Queen of the realm of Heaven. Passionately devoted to the pursuit of Wisdom and the possibilities of obtaining knowledge, even Magic was open to her, in the Temple Service. Could she leave her Temple home, her opportunities for growth, her idolized Priestess, to go into the environments of Nu-nah?

The thought seemed to her worse than death itself. "Every one has to die," she mused, "and I may as well die one time as another."

Then another thought came into her mind — Hermo.

He had begun to teach her the mysteries of his science of Astrology. Hermo, for whom she had a pure sisterly regard and who was so proud of her swift proficiency in his favorite study. And then she recalled the vision of the previous night when Hermo had shown to her clairvoyant eye his agitation at her impending doom.

"But if I become Nu-nah and Nu-nah becomes Sarthia, Hermo will never know the difference and thus be spared the pain of loving his young sister. And furthermore, Nu-nah has a lover to whom she is betrothed and would have married, ere this, but for her lingering malady, the superb young Prince Rathunor, whom I have never seen."

Ah! here was indeed a most dire complication. Love was a most mysterious and unknown emotion to her. She might hate Prince Rathunor and "then we would both wish I had died," and she half laughed to herself at the domestic comedy thus presented to her mind.

At this period, either as a reaction from the light thrown, or lighter thought upon her overwrought nature, or possibly from some subtle, potent influence emanating from the censer burning near her, Sarthia lapsed into sudden and most profound unconsciousness.

A few moments later — it seemed to Sarthia as if ages had intervened — she began a fierce struggle to awake. "Why, how is this?" she thought. She seemed enveloped in a dead wall of some kind. The brain, the heart, the infinite ramification of nerves in no way responded to her will and her utmost effort. Almost worn out with the unequal battle it began to dawn upon her that she was really endeavoring to animate the other body. "Am I becoming Nu-nah?" Yes, in the excitement of the moment she raised herself upon her couch and, resting upon her elbow, gazed upon the rigid form of what a moment before had been herself.

But her movement had startled a form beside the couch, some one who had approached, unobserved by Sarthia, during the interval of unconsciousness.

A young man who seemed to her the most God-like being she had ever beheld and perceiving her glance, with a low exclamation of joy, sprang toward her, clasped her hand in his, and turning her face upward, gazed with most passionate tenderness into her eyes.

"My Nu-nah, you will live," he murmured. "Do you know your Rathunor?"

Thrilled to suffocation by the love in his eyes, every atom of her soul vibrating to a new-born and overwhelming emotion, she felt herself slowly but surely losing control of her new body. With, however, one supreme effort she pressed the hand holding hers and returning the look in his eyes she gave one deep, quivering sigh and was gone.

When again she regained consciousness she was within her own body. Rathunor had vanished and the first slanting rays of the Moon were descending the last aperture.

It was midnight, and she found herself in communication with the Hierophant, who, from a different portion of the Sanctuary, was seriously regarding her and again reading her inmost thoughts.

A few moments before she had all but decided that she could not be Nu-nah, that death now, here in this Holy Sanctuary were better far than hundreds of years as a Princess of the realm of materiality. But, a new factor had now entered her being. A force, more subtle than all Wisdom, — more potent than life or eternity itself, — had transfused her soul — Love! Love, the first, the highest, the all-embracing force of the mighty Universe, and with this new love had been ushered also into being, Jealousy.

"Rathunor loved Nu-nah! Am I not a strange interloper? Was it not worse by my decision to rob Nu-nah of her lover than to deprive her of continued physical life?"

For, it seemed to her now, that life without love would be more than the agonies of the lowest hells. Then again, to live with Rathunor as his wife, while he all the time thought her to be Nu-nah, would be an incessant torture, keener and more intense than if she were chained by, as a third person, to behold him loving the actual Nu-nah in her own body.

"Holy Father and revered Hierophant," she moaned, "help me, I can not decide."

"My child," came the mental response to her call, "if you could be assured that Rathunor would love *you* in Nu-nah's body, would the decision be easy?"

"Aye, indeed, dear Father."

"Then rest assured it will be as you desire. We give you our sacred word that Rathunor will love *you*."

Then, raising his arm, as in benediction, he slowly repeated thrice, like an incantation, the words, "Rest in Peace," and, ere the echoes of his voice had died away, the soul of Sarthia had left forever its earthly abode and Temple.

# CHAPTER IV.

## WITHIN THE ADYTUM.

For several days, after floating from her body into the Astral world, Sarthia remained in a state of profound, dreamless slumber and then gradually passed into a condition of semi-consciousness with occasional fitful gleams of memory until one day she realized herself in close proximity to two persons engaged in earnest conversation and became fully aware of the momentous events that had just transpired and her present disembodied situation. And with a thrill indescribable she recognized the voice of Rathunor addressing the Hierophant.

"And so, most revered Father, all things are progressing favorably and toward a satisfactory culmination?" he said.

"Even so, my son," was the reply. "And yet," continued the Prince, "save the one momentary gleam of recognition, upon the first night of the ceremonies, the soul of the Princess Nu-nah, to all outward appearance, has left entirely. The body is sustained, apparently, by some magical process, the nature of which I do not understand."

"True, my son, but that need not disquiet you. The resources of Nature are many and far from being exhausted. But then, youth is naturally impatient. Did you so deeply love the Princess?"

At this point Sarthia would have withdrawn but she found that her desire to stay chained her to the spot, and glancing at the Hierophant she realized that her presence was known to him and that he wished her to remain.

The Prince mused thoughtfully for a few moments before replying and then said with a half sigh, "You know, O Father, that I myself did not particularly desire that marriage. From my earliest childhood I have been fond of my cousin and playfellow. As she matured I have admired, with family pride, her perfect beauty of form, her haughty spirit and her ability to rule. And yet, as you, who can so easily read the innermost secrets of the heart, must know I have not been able to discern the happiness for myself in this union that my soul would crave, or that you led me to expect in wedded love. If my ambition irresistibly impelled me to fill the external destinies of mankind, to become a monarch of unsurpassed power and magnificence, then would Nu-nah be the royal consort absolutely adapted for such pride and pomp. But, you know, O Father, all these things are as empty bubbles and child toys to one aspiring to become a Priest King, to him who hungers and thirsts, day and night for wisdom, for knowledge of the more inner secrets of Nature, guarded so jealously by the Priesthood but revealed by the very Gods themselves to those worthy to know and fit to use and assist in carrying out the plans and orderly workings of the very Universe itself.

"In form and feature Nu-nah's image meets my highest ideal, but when I would speak of the thoughts and ambitions upon which my soul dwells, then her cold look of incomprehension appalls me with the vast difference in our natures. Her thoughts can never penetrate the realm wherein my life-forces are all centered. Never have I experienced from her the response my love would crave."

"Have you then never at any time felt that Nu-nah's love for you could be trained and in time evolved to the plane whereby she would respond to you?"

"Nu-nah does not seem capable of the love of soul. She accepts me as a lover due her, and whose attention and presence gratify her pride and vanity. Never once, or perhaps only once, have I ever seen or imagined I saw a recognition of love, and that was the night of the full Moon, during the recent ceremonies. As, with your permission, I for a moment drew near the couch on which she reposed, she suddenly raised to a half-sitting position and seemed strangely startled by my presence. With a thrill of hope, that finally love was awakening, I sprang forward and spake anxiously and fondly to her. For the first time in all my life her glance vibrated to my heart's very core. My brain reeled with intoxication as she pressed my hand, and the love from her eyes burns now into my soul as I recall that one second of bliss. But, alas! she fell back into her former lifeless state and lingers so until I am in doubt if after all it were not some illusion connected with the wonderful Magic of that night."

"Nay," said the Hierophant, "I can assure you that what you experienced was *real* and that if this matter reaches a successful issue you will henceforward find in Nu-nah all that your soul desires, that ever will her eager spirit lead yours in the pursuit of knowledge and the highest wisdom."

Then the Hierophant turning, mentally addressed Sarthia, the unseen witness of the interview, "Am I not right in making this pledge for you to Rathunor? Think you we have also fulfilled our promise that Rathunor shall love you?"

But her heart was too full to reply. He then directed her attention to her location and surroundings and for the first time she became aware with amazement, almost terror, that she was within "THE SACRED ADYTUM — THE HOLY OF HOLIES," while the Hierophant and Rathunor were within an adjoining court and private apartment of the High Priest.

"My child," said the Hierophant in reply to her speechless inquiry as to the meaning of this wonder, "there are no barriers to the disembodied soul. This place, so religiously guarded, so inaccessible to the ordinary mortal, is open to any soul having passed a certain grade of initiation into the divine mysteries of Nature and attained unto that purity of heart whereby man may see his God.

"Tomorrow night, on the occasion of the new Moon, will be consecrated within this Holy Chamber, the union of your soul with that of Rathunor's and here also will be consummated that mystic transfer between your soul and that of Nu-nah's.

"And now, I leave you here while I accompany Rathunor. As you gradually lapse into the sweet silence of this Holy place, observe the meaning of some of the stupendous mysteries of Nature revealed here openly to the one having eyes to see and possessing the gift of understanding."

Her first sensation on being left alone was, that she was floating like the vapor of a breath upon the swaying wreaths of burning incense, and as she reclines thus in blissful repose there dawned upon her vision a view of the vast Temple in its absolute entirety. It assumed the strange outline of a gigantic human body, all its intricacies becoming orderly correspondencies of the human organism in its multitudinous ramifications. Then all the vast ceremonial of this body passed in review before her mind, each rite symbolic of some function, physical, mental and spiritual, and she marveled at the adaptability of the parts to each other and then to the grand whole.

But, above all, was she impressed by the depth in depths of meaning of this Sacred Adytum in its symbolic relation to the whole structure. However, ere she could tarry to reflect, the nature of the vision changed as if her eye had been turned suddenly from the lens of a Microscope to that of an immense Telescope. Before her view stretched the starry Zodiac, in outline, the same as its prototype, the human body — the Grand Temple. The Sun and its solar system corresponding to various vital functions in the human organism, but the crowning wonder of all came as she comprehended the relation which our planet, mother Earth, bore to the Grand Man of the skies, and her soul was overwhelmed as all the implications of this relation rushed in upon her being.

# CHAPTER V.

## THE TRANSFER.

According to the calculations made by the chief Astrologer Priest it was just at midnight that the conjunction of the luminaries took place in the Zodiacal sign belonging to the Moon. This union of the luminous orbs of the day and night is powerfully magical in its results.

The vibrations, set in motion by this mighty union of the positive and negative forces of Nature, react, not only upon the waters and the Earth, but the human family. Not only does the mighty ocean obey this wonderful influence in the ebb and flow of its tides, but the Earth, as she rotates upon her axis, obeys this mighty power and manifests in her depths and heights in her serpentine movement about the Sun.

Nature's laws are very exact and man, to become the Arbiter of his own destiny, must blend his energies in harmony with those of Nature.

Agreeable to appointment and the arrangements to be made it was necessary for the Hierophant and the Holy men of the Temple to assemble at an early hour, although the Transfer was not to take place until midnight.

Much preparation was necessary as a most momentous ceremony was to be performed this night; one that rarely ever was performed, owing to the fact that few of the Temple Priests were initiated into these sacred Magical Rites. They were too Sacred and Holy to be imparted to many, too dangerous for possible failures, too infinite in responsibilities accompanying such undertakings. Only those where the mind, soul and spirit, blended as one in their organism, were ever entrusted with the interior knowledge of the Sacred Adytum — The Holy of Holies.

Only the invocations were to be made, the chants and ceremonies belonging to the Holy Sanctuary were to be observed. The air was ladened with the sweet fragrance of incense and those subtle perfumes that are so delightful and enticing to the soul. Hours before the solemn Rites were to be performed, every part of the Holy Temple must be permeated with their magical and mystical influence.

The bodies of both Sarthia and Nu-nah lay in state before the Altar in the Holy Sanctuary, both robed and perfumed as if for burial.

The Hierophant of the Temple, the Priests and the Lay Priests, and the Priestesses with their Vestal Virgins, were now assembled in their respective places.

The hour of midnight had arrived. The chants now begun, set in vibration the spiritual forces that appeal only to the soul and spirit.

The subtle, silent will of the High Priest mentally commanded the presence of the departed spirit of Sarthia. At his bidding, she came floating toward him, and when within a certain distance from her inanimate body, she remained hovering over it. Most willingly and joyfully she came, knowing the promise of the High Priest would be realized when she became able to animate and control the body and mind of what was still Nu-nah's.

Rathunor was present at the urgent request of the Priest. He little dreamed why his presence was so much desired, and how he, who was so ignorant of the Temple rules and service, could be of any assistance.

A spark had been kindled within his very soul, the night that Sarthia found herself in Nu-nah's temple and for a moment consciously remembered and spoke, that had been burning deeper and deeper until now, it was ready to burst forth as an ever-living flame at the first breath of hope that this new emotion was of the soul — real and immortal.

Did he dare for a moment listen to the whispering of the interior self? Fear alone made him drive back and quell the monitions that sprang from within, for O, if they were only vain hopes could he survive the disappointment? The thought was crushing, and better, he thought, not to hope than believe an illusion.

The magnetic chord that yet held Nu-nah to her frail, prostrated body had not yet been severed. The unconscious soul hung or rather floated about its temple, apparently waiting for a stronger force from the interior realm to call it away.

The Hierophant stepped to the front of the Altar and, raising his hands, invoked the presence of the Gods and their assistance in this Sacred ceremony of making that Transfer of the spiritual life-line that binds the spirit to soul, and soul to body.

As the two souls hung suspended by these magnetic life-chords above their own bodies, through the magical influences of the Priests, the chants and music came closer and closer, as if drawn together by some strong magnetic attraction.

Sarthia, now, as well as Nu-nah, was unconscious of what was taking place. Nu-nah's was the natural unconscious state of an undeveloped soul in passing from the physical temple to the realms beyond, while Sarthia's was purposely induced by the magical will of the Operator.

The middle of the mystical hour had just been reached when the two life-lines met and blended for one single instant, then separated and, obeying the powerful wills of the Priests, became polarized in each other's body.

The magical invisible agency that had been animating the body of Sarthia was now withdrawn, and the soul of Nu-nah's gradually but faintly began to supply the animating force to revive and control the apparently lifeless form.

Sarthia's spiritual consciousness was not immediately allowed to return. The awakening must be gradual to her, for knowing what was being done, the joy and ecstacy of a prolonged life in the holy bonds of pure love with Rathunor would be disastrous if suddenly conveyed to her consciousness.

The High Priest, turning to Rathunor, said, "Our beloved pupil, return now to your usual duties, but fail not to return to the Temple a little before twelve o'clock tomorrow night."

Now the bodies of Sarthia and Nu-nah were removed to another part of the Temple. The Priestesses and Vestals, with the choir and musicians, were dismissed as the first part of the solemn and sacred Rites was over, but the Priests remained, never stopping in their magical work, for yet the vibrations of the new-born souls were not of sufficient strength and power to remain unassisted, especially that of Nu-nah's.

# CHAPTER VI.

## THE AWAKENING.

The constant presence of some of the Priests of the Temple had been near the bodies of Nu-nah and Sarthia continuously for the last twenty-four hours, and by their magic assistance the vibrations of the souls to their new tenements grew stronger and quite harmonious.

The hour of midnight was again near at hand. The reviving forms of the two young girls were again brought into the Holy Sanctuary of the Temple and placed in front of the Altar and the Hierophant who had already taken his position.

The Priestesses of the Temple with their Vestals were quietly and solemnly wending their way to their usual places. The choir had begun to chant the opening service when Rathunor with one of the Priests approached with slow and measured strides as if a false movement would disturb the solemnity of this midnight's mystic silence.

As they approached the spot where the two bodies lay, there was a perceptible movement, as of consciousness in the silent form of Nu-nah.

Just as the distant chimes pealed forth their announcement of the midnight hour the Hierophant arose and stepped forth to the front of the Altar and, at a silent signal, there broke forth, as of one voice, the low-distant strains of the most enchanting music. The voices and the tones from the musical instruments were so harmoniously and wonderfully blended that the result was magically effective. The strains increased in volume — they seemed to approach nearer and nearer — until the whole edifice resounded and re-echoed as though filled with one vast orchestra sounding forth the Anthem of Creative Life, "We Praise Thee, O God."

This enchanting music continued for some time, then gently died away until only the breathings of music could be heard, when the Hierophant raised his hands as if in supplication. The solemn, awful stillness of the hour was awe-inspiring.

Once, twice, thrice, the voice of the Hierophant resounded throughout the Sanctuary as he thus spoke to their souls:

"Arise, O ye daughter of Isis, come forth and again enter the daily lives of a Vestal and a Princess. Many years now are granted to your service, and now that you have both been beyond the dividing line of this and the other plane, your lives henceforth should be guided and influenced by that experience."

At this he descended from the Altar and took the helpless hand of Sarthia to magically convey to the silent, lifeless body the electric forces of life.

Turning to Rathunor, who stood near, beckoning him to his side, he took his hand and led him to that which *was* Nu-nah's body, and gently raising the apparently lifeless hand of the silent form placed it within that of Rathunor's. The effect was indeed magical.

Rathunor was held spell-bound, the thrilling sensations, the emotions that sprang forth from the heart were electrifying. He could feel the tense vibrations passing from his hand to that of her body, the source of which he could not fathom nor understand, and little did he care at that moment when he perceived the slight tremor that was creeping over the heretofore lifeless form of his Princess Nu-nah.

Here, Rathunor would have been overcome by his emotions of joyful bliss and thrown himself prostrate at the feet of the Priest in thankful gratitude for the restoration to life of his lovely Nu-nah, had not the Hierophant just at this moment laid his hand upon Rathunor's shoulder saying, "My child, have you become unconscious of the place and the occasion, and the solemn promise you gave me to bravely follow my instructions without a show of weakness. Let not an outward manifestation of your feelings escape you again. Are you yourself again?"

With a mighty effort of his will Rathunor commanded an outward calm at least, but he could not speak, he could only bow his head in assurance and being told to retain the hand of Nu-nah, the Priest continued audibly, "In the name of the Almighty and ever-living God I now join these two souls as one. May their consciousness of this, their soul-union, dawn upon their outward memory as time proceeds, and then journey together in conscious union on the eternal path of progress to the Divine Throne of God. Amen! Amen!"

Rathunor heard but did not understand and being overcome by the silent over-powering influence surrounding him, fell insensible to the floor beside the reviving form of Nu-nah.

As soon as he had been conveyed to an outer court, the Hierophant again continued. Turning his attention to Sarthia, mentally he called three times, "Nu-nah, Nu-nah, Nu-nah, henceforth you shall be known as Sarthia the Vestal. May the guardian angels that have been placed over your reviving body, keep and hold the soul with it until health of body and strength of mind returns. God bless our new-found Vestal. Amen."

As the last echo of the Priest's voice died away the music burst in a joyful song of praise, and continued until the bodies of each of the young girls were removed. Sarthia's to that formerly occupied by the Vestal, and Nu-nah's to that of the home of the Princess.

Rathunor soon revived in the fresh air of the outer court and now being summoned by a messenger from the Hierophant presented himself again before him.

"My son," said the High Priest, "go to the home of the Princess and remain, either with, or near her until three cycles of seven shall pass by. At the end of twenty-one days you may return to your own home and enter the accustomed life of a Prince, until that time shall come when the Prince of the world shall enter the path that leads to a King of Wisdom," and with a fervent press of the hand and a benediction for his soul's welfare he bid him good-night and retired from the Holy Sanctuary.

# CHAPTER VII.

## A VISIT TO THE CHIEF ASTROLOGER.

A few weeks after the preceding ceremonies, a messenger announced to the Astrologer Priest that the Priestess sought an interview.

Hermo was at his post making the usual, daily calculations for the Priest. As the Priestess entered, Hermo arose, and was about to withdraw, when the Priestess, by a wave of her hand, gave him to understand his presence was required.

The Priestess began, "O, most Venerated Father, I come again to ask assistance, with your astrological knowledge, in behalf of Sarthia. The memory of the past seems to be entirely blotted out. Is there any aspect showing that memory will return, and if not, at what time do the planets indicate a commencement of the training of the mind that will bring a successful issue in spiritual things? We will have to commence with her as a child and train the body, mind and soul to Vestal Service."

The Astrologer turned to Hermo and said, "Hear you the request of our Priestess here? Make note, and see at what time the planets point favorably to the initiation of our new Sarthia into the Temple Service of Isis."

"How is our new Sarthia?" inquired the Priest.

"Nothing, as yet," answered the Priestess, "But that does not disturb my hope and faith that she will become all that we wish and desire of her, and instead of having but one Vestal we shall have two, for ere long Nu-nah will also be numbered among our Vestals, and Rathunor as one of our Priests."

Thanking the Priest for his promised service the Priestess withdrew.

The Astrologer returned to his studies and was soon absorbed with them, when, suddenly he turned to Hermo and said, "Hermo, I shall place Sarthia under your special tutelage as soon as she is ready to commence her studies in Astrology."

The suddenness of the Priest's remarks quite confused the young scribe and set him to seriously thinking. Strange thoughts came into his mind, "why should Sarthia *not* continue her studies with me, why would she become a special and *not* a fellow student?"

He could not account for these strange thoughts that had been excited within his mind, and the rest of the hours of work did not show the usual amount accomplished.

At an early hour the next night, before Hermo had arrived for his night's work, the Astrologer Priest sent for the Priestess. She hastily responded to the summons feeling there was some very important news to be received. As soon as she entered the Priest said, "Most noble Priestess, I find by the calculations made, that not before another month may our infant child, Sarthia, be initiated, as a pupil, into the Temple of Isis. Two days before the full Moon the spiritual rays will be most active and potent, and being of so harmonious a nature we may hope for the most satisfactory results. The task will be slow and require much patience, my Priestess, for the hereditary tendencies of the brain, that have so far influenced that soul's life and experiences, will have to be polarized in other channels and gradually awakened to consciousness. The life of the body it has been animating in past years was not of such a nature as to mature a healthy soul.

"The work now, with our new Sarthia, is with the Soul, to make it equal to the brain that has been cultivated and enlarged in spiritual ways; while with Nu-nah, the work will be in arousing and developing that brain to the conscious response of the matured soul. Do I make myself plain to you? In my young pupil, Hermo, we will have a most valuable assistant in our work with Sarthia, for I have discovered that the divine relation of brother and sister exists between them. They are blest with being the emanations from the same divine state and children of the same spiritual parents. I spoke to Hermo of Sarthia last night, at the same time *willing* that my new discovery might be imparted to his soul, which I could see had been partially accomplished.

"We will allow them often in each other's society, and that holy love of brother of sister, and sister of brother, which can only be kindled in the outer heart when this spiritual relation exists.

"This will soon be recognized by each of them, and this alone will be a most potent influence in nourishing and teaching the soul of Sarthia. Nothing lies in Sarthia's path that portends serious evil for many years to come. Therefore, my good Priestess, take new hope and courage, and not many Moons will grow and wane before an inward pride will be born for your new Vestal."

The Priestess retired after thanking him most cordially, and could hardly conceal her emotions of joy and rapture until she was safe in her own apartments, where she could give full vent, in tears and cries of joy and gratitude.

As soon as all traces of the effects, which this knowledge had produced, were erased, and she became perfectly calm and composed, she sought Sarthia's chamber. The young girl was reclining upon a couch that had been drawn near the window, apparently much absorbed in studying the heavens. Scarcely did she notice the presence of the Priestess until she knelt beside her and said, "What thoughts are being born in my Sarthia's mind as she views the mighty heavens above with its millions of silent monitors, awaiting our pleasure to read and understand? Are they speaking to my darling child? Do you hear their silent voices and feel their subtle and powerful influences upon you?"

The young girl did not reply immediately. The body was still very weak and feeble, the mind was as one just awakening from a prolonged slumber.

"My beloved Priestess, did you speak to me of the stars, those loving lights in the heavens? They do seem to speak, but I can not understand and know what they say. Do you, dear Mother, and can you tell me?"

This first ray of awakening memory was more radiant to the Priestess than a thousand stars could have produced if all their rays could have blended into one. But calmness was her external bearing. Seldom any manifestation of an unusual emotion, was permitted to find an outward expression either in manner or speech. She had attained that perfect command of herself that neither joy nor sorrow, good nor evil, praise nor blame, could unbalance the perfect poise and tranquillity of her developed Soul.

"My Sarthia," replied the Priestess, "I can not know what they are saying to *you*, but they do speak to me. They

tell me that life is immortal, that the growth and the progress of the soul are eternal, that we may know and read
their language while in these bodies if we try; then as we
draw nearer and nearer to them, as our souls grow and
become familiar with their teachings, we can know them
as well, if not better, than our Astrologer Priests do, also
as well as your brother Hermo is learning to do."

"My — brother — Hermo," and there was a perceptible light of intelligence in the eyes for a moment.

The Priestess was not speaking to the mind, but to the
soul, at the same time willing to find a response there. The
mere words availed nothing to her, only in so much as
they expressed the longings and desires of the interior
self.

As Sarthia said no more, the Priestess arose and,
moving quietly about the room, gave a few directions and
cautions to those in attendance, then presently withdrew.

That night was passed by the Priestess in her own private chamber, not in sleep and rest, but actively and earnestly engaged in silent prayer for her new-born children,
Nu-nah, Sarthia and Rathunor.

# CHAPTER VIII.

## PRINCESS NU-NAH.

The morning following the Priestess' visit to Sarthia's apartments, she sent a messenger to inquire for the welfare of Princess Nu-nah.

She was reported to have slept well, seemed much stronger, but a peculiar change had taken place during her almost fatal illness. She spoke strangely, almost weirdly at times, which excited much comment and anxiety amongst her immediate friends and relatives.

The Princess had been a general favorite and much admired by those occupying the same station in life with herself; but by those who were subject to her commands and rule, she was looked upon as cold, stern, and heartless, kind in her way when obeyed, but the slightest disobedience brought scornful reproaches and often punishment.

The Priestess, knowing the source of the peculiar change spoken of, felt that all was well. No other attention than the presence of Rathunor was needed. The developed soul of the Vestal Sarthia would soon come into control of the brain she was now trying to find expression through.

Then, too, the organs of the brain that Sarthia's soul would naturally vibrate, had never become active, nor developed; they, as it were, were dormant, fast asleep, awaiting the pulsating vibrations of the spiritual influx to give them life and usefulness. While those that had been so fully developed in the brain, by the life of the Princess, found no corresponding vibrations from the soul.

Truly, a strange commingling of the two opposing forces, and one in which time was required to bring about perfect adjustment.

The High Priest had commanded all visitors to be excluded, except Rathunor, who was to have access at all times, and as the Hierophant's word was that of God to them, so, purely from a religious standpoint, they were strictly obeyed. While the Priestess and others of the Temple knew the secret of the Priest's strict injunctions, they likewise knew that none of Sarthia's associates dared approach, lest their presence would too suddenly awake to consciousness the slumbering soul, before the brain had yet fully responded and vibrated to the new animating spark of life.

Rathunor, most of all, observed the change in the Princess; at the slightest touch there was a response within — his very presence struck the chords of sympathy that existed between them. This was, to him, a very unaccountable change. In all his life association with Nu-nah these emotions, that now seemed to spring from the soul, had never before been experienced. He was very much inclined to attribute it to an abnormal sympathy aroused by her sickness and terrible suffering. Still, the words of the High Priest haunted him and the feelings born from within, on the night of the solemn Rites at the Temple, could not be vanished by any amount of reasoning; still he would not allow such thoughts to be nourished by the slightest hope — much less be watered by the spirit of faith and allowed to grow. Although Rathunor was brave in external pain, and daringly courageous in acts of chivalry, he was an infant when subject to disappointment. Here was the battle of self going on.

"Have I the strength and manly courage to bear the disappointment born from a delusive hope? Not yet." So he suffered and heeded not the whisperings from within, until he could not endure it any longer, when he sought the presence of the Hierophant for advice and enlightenment. Scarcely able to hold in check his impatience he burst forth without the recognition due the superior presence of a High Priest.

"O, most Holy and Revered Father, tell me, am I wrong in not listening to the monitions that are racking my inmost being? May I hope the love that is growing within my soul will be surely recognized and reciprocated by Nu-nah on her return to physical health? Is this love a vain delusion on my part, an imagination born from sympathies that will vanish as soon as health is restored and we enter the whirl of the social world again? If it is in thy power, O Father, tell me the truth. Repeat thy assuring words once more, and I will be guided by them in the future, and never again allow the shadow of doubt to cross the threshold of my mind."

"My child," said the High Priest, "once more I assure you of the loving response of Nu-nah's soul and mind, as soon as she is herself again. But, mark you well, at the return of consciousness, be not rash in any of your words or acts; remember, her return to life is as a new-born babe — weak, tender and easily impressed by stronger minds and wills than its own. You are the stronger at present, and all patience and indulgence are exacted from you. Let her imaginations and fancies play as they will for awhile; yours must be calm, loving, sympathetic and unwavering in hope and faith that all will eventually be well; and again, I assure you that not many years shall pass before you will enter the path and the life your soul is now longing for. Princess Nu-nah will more than compensate you for all the kind attentions you now bestow upon her in the guiding, teaching and leading your soul in the paths to spiritual knowledge and the spiritual life, while still inhabiting the physical form.

"The hungerings of your soul shall be more than satisfied by her ministering spirit. The interior consciousness will gradually dawn upon you both, but to Nu-nah first." Then, taking Rathunor by the hand, he continued, "Doubt no more, my child, have faith in the Infinite Wisdom that guides and directs the struggling soul through the intricate ways of evolution up to the final consciousness of Immortal Life. God be with and bless you."

Rathunor had no words to express his gratitude. But they would have been useless to the Hierophant, for the new-born light that shone forth, though dimly, was more to the Priest than a world of words.

He merely looked, bowed, and with a fervent pressure of the hand, was gone from the presence of the Holy Priest. As he retraced his steps toward the home of Princess Nu-nah, a holy calm pervaded his whole being; his doubts fled as an enemy; his excitement was transformed into tranquil earnestness; a sublime sense of the realities of life filled his brain, and a willingness to await the progress and development, that time would bring forth and mature, possessed him, until he was so changed that he scarcely recognized himself.

Was this change volitional?

# CHAPTER IX.

## THE INITIATION.

Days of weary watching, and toilsome care that the new-born Vestal would not be misled in her awakening thoughts, were necessary. The body needed but little care other than the proper nourishment and attention of any one in usual health. Sarthia's physical organism had not become depleted by disease and suffering, and the disorganization that had commenced was checked by the magical agent that had been placed over it, even before Sarthia had entirely left it.

The lethargy was more mental than physical. It was that semi-consciousness that precedes sleep, or that one sometimes experiences when awakened suddenly out of a deep, profound slumber.

The Priestess visited her many times throughout the day when she could spare the time from her duties in the Temple. In the course of a few days Sarthia was able to be assisted in short walks about the halls and corridors, but took little heed of things about her. Day by day, the body grew stronger and a new light began to dawn in the eyes and shone upon the countenance of the fair young girl.

In the meantime, Hermo had been apprised by the Astrologer Priest of the true relation existing between himself and Sarthia. His joy knew no bounds, for neither his heart nor soul had ever thrilled with the love of mother, sister, or kindred. It had been his misfortune to be deprived of his parents before his young mind and heart could be moved by the tender emotions of love, but now it needed no more than the Priest's revelations to kindle into flaming fires that something, he knew not what, that had been smoldering in his bosom all his life.

Now, the Astrologer's words were clear and the cause of the strange thoughts that were excited in his mind was revealed. Over and over he asked himself, "Can I wait to see my beloved sister?"

His impatience became equal with his joy, and days that had before passed as moments now seemed as ages. One morning, much to the Priestess' surprise, a messenger announced that Hermo desired an interview with her in the waiting-room below. The Priestess descended to where Hermo was waiting and, with a questioning look in her face, clasped his hand in a firm but anxious manner, inquired, "Is all well with our young Astrologer, Hermo, this morning. Does he bring tidings from our revered Father? Has any new testimony been given by the stars that portends evil to our Sarthia?"

Hermo stood in mute astonishment. "How could the Priestess receive such forebodings from his presence when his whole being was throbbing with pulsations of unbounded happiness," he thought.

"Nay, my dear Priestess, quite the reverse. Has not our worthy Father acquainted you with my new-found joy, my Love — my Sister? Know you not the divine relation that exists between Sarthia and myself? The hours have seemed days since this knowledge was revealed to me and I now beg to see my new sister and walk with her and yourself upon the lawn in the private grounds of the Temple. Can my request be granted, O Priestess?"

She still retained his hand and, again pressing it warmly between her own, said, "Our brave and noble Hermo deserves this blessing as a reward for his honest toil alone in his struggle for Truth and Knowledge. Yes, my dear Hermo, I was made aware of the relation between you and our new Sarthia and have been anxious for this moment to arrive when you would be sent to escort Sarthia in her daily walks about the grounds, but I caution you to be guarded in your words. Remember she is yet but an infant and must be taught as a child. Remain here and I will go and bring Sarthia thither and we will walk together."

It was not long before the Priestess, Sarthia and her attendant appeared. The Priestess was leading Sarthia and as they approached Hermo placed her hand in that of his saying, "Sarthia, I place you in the care and protection of your brother Hermo."

"Hermo! Hermo!! My brother Hermo?" said Sarthia.

To the penetrating eyes of the Priestess and Hermo the light of consciousness was momentarily seen and to the clairvoyant vision of the Priestess a startling scene was beheld. The vibrations of soul to soul, the love that had been kindled in Hermo's heart and soul went out with such intensity that it aroused into a vivid activity the slumbering soul of Sarthia, and the brain, being already so finely tuned to the higher vibrations of the Spirit, responded at once.

The fresh air, the green grass, the beautiful flowers and shrubbery, with the inspiring presence of Hermo, were like magic to quicken the pulsations of body and mind and bring to her cheek and eyes the flush of health and life. Not much of the conversation was directed to

Sarthia, but when reference to the stars was made, she instantly inquired, "Brother Hermo, do the stars speak to you, and do you know what they say? Our lovely Priestess here can read them, and how much I would love to speak with them, too."

"I will teach you how some day, my sister, as soon as you are able to commence your studies."

"Will that be soon?"

"Yes, in a short time; so soon as you become an attendant in The Temple of Isis."

Sarthia was silent, and the Priestess reminded them it was time to return, — Sarthia to her room and Hermo to his studies, while the Priestess' presence was required in the Temple.

These walks continued daily with most satisfactory results to the Priestess and the Hierophant. All fears of the perfect harmonizing of the new soul to the body of Sarthia were allayed. The animating spark of life was growing stronger and the vibrations from soul to body were complete; not with consciousness, but that involuntary vibratory exchange that exists with the majority of the people that make up the earth's human family. As only the higher portion of the brain of Sarthia had been active the soul must necessarily manifest itself through those organs. Often, were the much beloved Priestess, Hermo and Sarthia's attendants, surprised at her expressions and profound questions on spiritual subjects.

It was nearing the time when Sarthia was to take her initiatory step as a Vestal in the Temple of Isis. In fact, only one more day intervened before the ceremony was to take place. As the incidents relative to the transfer were known to all the Temple attendants, it was looked forward to with much silent rejoicing and gratitude that they had not been robbed of their lovely Vestal who always was held in sacred esteem by them all.

All had been notified to prepare for the Initiatory service — the music, chants, and ceremonies sacred to this occasion, must be in readiness. The night had arrived; the fair Goddess of the night shone forth in all her radiant splendor, seemingly conscious, that she was shedding forth the magnetic influence necessary for the sacred Rites now about to be performed. It had almost reached the Zenith when the solemn march of the Priestesses, Vestals and attendants that were to conduct Sarthia to the Holy Sanctuary of the Temple started. The Priestess walked beside Sarthia. Sarthia was clothed in pure spotless linen, her head was bare with the exception of a wreath of laurel leaves that rested lightly upon her flowing hair. In her hands she carried a white-bound volume which contained the songs, chants, litany and regime for the Vestals of the Temple.

Just as they reached the door, the High Priest arose, and simultaneously the music burst forth in joyful strains that spoke welcome, courage and love to the heart of Sarthia. When they reached the foot of the altar, where stood the Hierophant, Sarthia knelt upon a velvet cushion at his feet. The music ceased while the High Priest stood with uplifted hands in silent prayer. At a signal, the choir began chanting the Litany. Sarthia was bidden to rise, when the Priest, in measured and solemn tones, addressed her:

"Do you come to pledge yourself to Temple Service? Is it your desire to become a Vestal of Isis? Do you take the pledge of celibacy to the virgin Rites of the Temple; your time, energy and purpose to be devoted to the duties that devolve upon a Vestal?"

The low, clear voice of Sarthia was heard throughout the Sanctuary as she bowed and answered in assent.

"So be it, my holy virgin. I now commit your soul to the Guardian Angels of this Sacred Sanctuary to guide, guard and protect your budding soul to perfect at-one-ment with its divine center, that you may inherit immortal life while yet with us. Amen!"

Sarthia opened the book within her hands and, kissing its pages which she had already subscribed to, handed it to the High Priest. He took it, and held it in his left, while he placed his right hand upon her head, and said:

"I bid thee welcome, my Vestal Sarthia, and commend thy soul to the Gods above, that ever keep watch o'er the children of earth. God bless thee. Amen! Amen!"

Then, as if they were voicing the words of the Hierophant, the chants grew louder, the music poured forth in grander tones as though to join the invisible hosts above in praise to God most high.

The ceremony was over and Sarthia was conducted back to her chamber, a Vestal of The Temple of Isis. The occult powers that had been evoked in behalf of Sarthia soon became manifest in her daily life. The zeal and zest with which she pursued her studies and the understanding of their interior meanings were sufficient evidence of her teacher's inspiring influence. She was soon placed under her brother Hermo's instruction in astronomical and astrological lore, and here also displayed a proficiency in learning that surprised Hermo and delighted the Astrologer Priests. At Temple Service she was all devotion and, as an Attendant, ever true and faithful. The brother and sister became devotedly attached to each other and the Priestess often observed this attachment, which sent a pang through her heart, lest such joy and happiness might not be granted Hermo for the remainder of his life. Then instantly would she offer a silent prayer that such supreme happiness would be theirs throughout eternity.

# CHAPTER X.

## THE PRINCESS' WEDDING.

The Princess' recovery was very slow, owing to the great depletion of the physical body during her recent illness. Much care and attention were bestowed upon her by her royal friends. All the luxury which wealth alone could procure, and the kindly influences of loving associates were brought to bear to speedily hasten the restoration of their Princess to her former health and spirits. Health was slowly but surely gaining the ascendency, but the spirits of heart and mind were not of that buoyant, external nature that she formerly displayed.

With her return to health, demands of a social nature were made upon her. She enjoyed pleasures but a seriousness attended her every movement that much annoyed her friends. The attendants and servants were excited to wonder at her kind and thoughtful interests of them — while many thought it was due to her weak physical condition, others remarked, how much the Princess' sickness had improved her. Those that before feared her, now began to love and seek to please and serve her.

Rathunor was a daily visitor, and remembering the advice and instructions of the Hierophant he was calm, silent, and patient in his attentions to her and apparently took no heed of her fancies and strange conversation. She would constantly plan amusements and social entertainments on a grand scale, but with such a seriousness of purpose that it quite annoyed Rathunor at times and caused him to wonder if this was really his former Nu-nah.

While the annoyance came purely from the external, there was an interior attraction that was, irresistibly, holding him spell-bound to her side. His happiness now was greatest when they sat, rode or walked in silence. Little did he dream, while in that silence which so enraptured him, the soul of Nu-nah was blending and drawing the electric life-essence from his own to hers. That interchange was going on wherein there is no robbery, but an inter-blending of the magnetic and electric life-forces that cause to spring into activity the harmonious vibrations of a complete whole, and the reaction upon both brain and the physical organism was health, contentment and happiness that rises above all external cares, sorrows and discords.

Although the soul of the, now known, Princess was highly developed it could find but few responsive echoes from the dormant spiritual organs of the brain. These she must arouse to sensitiveness and action. It was this that gave rise to the peculiar ideas, expressed in her conversation, that so mystified her friends. Visitors soon began to pour in upon her congratulations, presents and invitations to once again enter the gilded salons of fashion and the round of amusements that are the daily life of a favorite Princess. To all she gave a modest, quiet reply, neither accepting nor rejecting their attentions, which left them in wondering doubt at times of her sanity.

In the midst of some grand occasion she would be suddenly missed and on being sought out would be found concealed in some pleasant nook, or even out in the open air, or beside an open window, absorbed in meditation or gazing into the heavens. When her attention was attracted she would start and, with a strange, far-away look in her eyes that would indicate to a superficial observer she had been asleep, would allow herself to be led back and enter the festivities of the hour.

With all their efforts they could not enthuse her with the excitement and merriment surrounding her. But, if any one should become serious and express thoughts that appealed to the interior, she was all attention and the questions that were so ready when such an opportunity afforded showed plainly that, although present in body, the soul and interests were in other realms and spheres than this.

No one but Rathunor could hold her attention for any length of time. With him she was animated, and charmingly beautiful and joyous and would, with some enthusiasm, enter into the pleasantries of the hour which brought to her face the charming attraction of natural beauty. Behind those orbs of vision there seemed to shine forth a light that was more radiant than the gorgeously brilliant illuminations of the salons. Her beautiful face, her perfect form and bearing, made her the center of attraction and she was much sought after. But, as soon as she was induced to leave Rathunor's side, that which made her presence so irresistibly attractive and radiant before, faded out.

Thus time passed on, and as health returned, Prince Rathunor pressed his suit. There was now, no apparent reason why he could not claim his promised bride and make the Princess Nu-nah his own. His more earnest friends cautioned him to wait further developments and, in an undertone, reminded him of the peculiar and unnatural bearing of the Princess at times. They were sure, in time, their once lovely Princess would be herself again. Rathunor listened, knowing their kindly interest sprang from good motives, but he was silent — he could not speak for none would understand. The yearnings of his heart and soul would not be quelled by any outward show.

While to the world Nu-nah was a source of mystical wonder, to Rathunor she was his stay and comfort. He needed no further evidence and assurance of Nu-nah's love for him. Too often had he experienced the response from within to her silent pleadings for light, truth and wisdom. The attraction of the outer world was losing its fascination for him, the longings from within grew stronger and more clamorous for outward expression until, one day, he advanced the subject of astrology to the Princess Nu-nah. For an instant, her whole being was illuminated by that mysterious light — for a single moment the soul arose to the supremacy of the brain and found a faint glimmering expression that was visible to Rathunor's ever-watchful eye.

"Astrology, my Rathunor, fascinates me with its name and the wonders and mysteries it is said to reveal. Do you think those Astrologer Priests of the Temple know whereof they speak, and do they read the stars and gain from them the wisdom they are said to possess?"

Here was the first opportunity to present these sacred subjects to Nu-nah's mind. He tried to think and, feeling that the present excitement of the brain's higher organs, was of a temporary nature, he was really at a loss what to say that would be most effective and impress itself indelibly upon her awakening brain.

"Yes, my dear Nu-nah, I believe they do possess the knowledge they claim and, I also am convinced that much of that wisdom and knowledge is gained through their understanding the laws of astrology. Those celestial bodies in our heavens were not placed there by our Divine Creator without a purpose. I believe they have an influence upon us that can be learned, defined and utilized by those who study and know this influence through astronomy and astrology. Nu-nah what is that which produces the interior longings to know? Is it not that there is something to know — something that our common brains can not grasp and analyze? Do you not think that silent, yet persistent, monitor which lies concealed somewhere within our being is excited to action from some source other than our outward selves, and that longing to go out must be accounted for by a something without that calls and attracts us to it? May this not be the stars that we see twinkling and motioning to us as we gaze into the midnight heavens?"

He stopped, wondering what the effect of his words would be, when, to his amazement, there appeared a more vivid consciousness in her eyes and features than he had ever seen since her return to physical health and, taking new hope from this manifestation, he continued, "Do you love the social world longer? Is there not that longing, too, within your bosom for something more real, more ennobling than the pastimes of worldly pleasures?"

At the mention of the worldly things, the light from her eyes died out and was gone. Rathunor said no more but silently thanked God that he had for those few moments assisted the soul of Nu-nah to vibrate, too; and had set in motion the vitalizing currents to the spiritual portion of the brain and earnestly prayed that this might be the beginning of many opportunities that were to follow.

Realizing that only he could arouse the dormant organs of her spiritual brain, he became more anxious than ever to have her constantly in his company. He again pressed his suit and the day for the wedding-nuptials was to be at once submitted to the Astrologer.

Rathunor again sought the Astrologer Priest for advice. He wished to know when the stars would point most favorably toward such a momentous event. This, the Astrologer was not long in finding out and soon conveyed the news to Rathunor that at an early date such might be consummated. As the Prince arose to go the Priest took his hand and said, "My child, in taking the Princess Nunah as your wife, you obey the holy intuitions of the soul and not only will you be united in soul but in body and mind. I wish you the eternal bliss that attends all who are truly mated. Farewell, my child; my blessings go with you."

Rathunor was too much absorbed in other things to understand the mysterious words of the Priest, but notwithstanding this the seed had been again sown that would sometime spring up unannounced and unexpected.

The announcement of the wedding was soon made and invitations sent out, far and near. Congratulations poured in from every source, although some would have refused, had they been true to their own sentiments, for the remarkable and unaccountable change which had taken place during her terrible malady was too evident to be altogether right and should be righted before the Prince should make the Princess his wife.

Rathunor was satisfied, never forgetting the Hierophant's sacred words, and none other need be consulted. In their silent hearts they wished the wedding might be private and the holy ceremony of the Temple be performed by the High Priest. This, of course, could not be owing to the station and position they occupied in life, for the lives of a Princess and Prince are not wholly their own, so to the public they must bow and pay obeisance.

Preparations for the wedding commenced at once, for it was to be a grand affair. Nothing was to be spared that would add beauty and grandeur to the occasion. Extravagant expenditures were indulged in, until money seemed at a loss to supply more. The trousseau was exquisitely magnificent and, on the wedding night, the beaming radiance of the countenance of the Princess was neither dimmed by the rich silks, nor the rare, priceless laces and lovely jewels that glittered and sparkled with the living spark of life within them, that adorned her form.

Never a bride so fair; never a couple so happy. It was that quiet, subtle happiness, which permeates the very atmosphere about them and leaves its traces in every susceptible heart that breathes it.

# CHAPTER XI.

## THE RETIREMENT.

After the wedding the Prince and Princess were, from necessity, drawn within the whirl of social pleasures with attentions in the way of entertainments, court suppers, balls, drawing-room receptions, etc. The interior longings were compelled to creep into the background until the external was gratified to exhaustion. The Princess' seriousness departed for a time and they were very happy in the round of pleasures that were planned for them. But as time sped on they began to grow weary of the show, pomp and shallowness of external life. The seeds that had been sown in Rathunor's heart and brain, and that which he had aroused in Nu-nah's slumbering, spiritual organs of her brain, had taken root and now began to spring forth into activity, first as weariness of the superficial pleasures of society, then a desire to gradually withdraw from this life into a more quiet and secluded one, where they might listen to the inner voices and gain pleasure, as well as knowledge, from this source.

The Prince anxiously awaited another opportunity

for speaking to Princess Nu-nah on spiritual subjects. The Hierophant had given him to understand that at no distant day Nu-nah would become interested in spiritual things and be his teacher. He had not been made aware of the transfer — that was to be revealed to him by Nu-nah herself. He had begun to wonder how and where Nu-nah's spiritual awakening would take place when an opportunity presented itself in a most unexpected manner.

One lovely evening they were taking a stroll about the grounds of their castle, when the full Moon arose in a flood of light, it rose higher, fuller, until the whole world seemed bathed in her magical beauty and in order to longer enjoy her light and magnetic influence the Prince suggested a longer walk. Unconsciously they chose the path that led them towards the Temple, which was only a short distance from their home. As they neared the Temple distant strains of music attracted their attention. They listened, and it seemed to speak in the plaintive tones of a hungering soul; they hastened their steps until they had quite reached the private grounds of the Temple of Isis, Nu-nah was in advance of Rathunor, being irresistibly drawn by some invisible power, when she suddenly stopped and clasping his arm, as within a vice, cried out, "My Rathunor, do you hear that music; what is it? I have heard it before, but where, O, where? How came I to know the chants and music of the Temple Service?"

They were held spell-bound to the spot, when the Prince was warned, by the trembling and the gradual loosening of Nu-nah's hand upon his arm, to quit the spot at once. The Prince placed his arm about her waist to support her as he urged their return home, but she stood immovable apparently chained by the magical power of some invisible force.

Stronger grew the mystical power of the spell until the

Princess seemed compelled to rush madly on and into the Temple, if the Prince had not held her back in a firm grasp, and at the same time trying to attract her attention by his words. "Come, my darling, let us retrace our steps and as we walk I will tell you all I know about what you have heard."

"O, my Rathunor, speak to me quickly before I have time to forget. I can not remember this long, yet it as a recurrence of a vivid dream. Tell me while I am awake, where I have been. I saw, and felt, and know I was there — there in the Sacred Sanctuary of that Temple. O, that I might go again and remain there forever to listen to that enchanting music and the solemn heavenly voices of that choir."

A quiver ran through her whole frame and with a mournful cry she fell fainting in the arms of Rathunor. Here his innate born courage and bravery sustained him, and instantly there flashed into his mind the words he had once heard the High Priest use while passing his hands over an insensible form. So, gently laying her inanimate body upon the grass, he repeated in slow, but firm and commanding tones these words:

"Return, O soul, to thy physical body. Return, I command thee, and reanimate this lifeless tenement of your soul. Come, come, I command thee, come."

Scarcely had the last words been uttered when a movement of the hands and limbs announced to Rathunor the return of life. She was soon able to rise and, being supported by the Prince, they slowly wended their way back to the castle. She walked as in a dream, but as her step was stately and firm, the Prince did not become alarmed until he had her safe in her room, when the extent of the occurrence dawned upon him and then he hurriedly called her maid and sent at once to dispatch a servant for their physician. Nu-nah had become quite herself before the Doctor came and after he had administered a little palliative, withdrew saying, "The Princess will soon be well. It was only the result of fatigue induced by the constant excitement of social pleasures."

The Prince was silent and, seeing the Princess was so comfortable, he retired to his own apartments with strict injunctions, he should be notified at once if any symptoms of the prostration should appear. When once within his private chamber he threw himself down in a chair and fell into a profound study. Over and over he reviewed the incidents of the evening. "What was there in that music that so enchanted Nu-nah? What did she see and hear that revived a faint memory of something in the past? What magical force was it that drew her so irresistibly toward the Temple? What produced that quiver which preceded her falling insensible into his arms?"

He was half inclined to blame the Priests for it all, for he knew something of the power of magic and its psychologic effect. The more he reasoned the farther he wandered from a solution. Now he mused, "If that had been the beautiful Vestal, Sarthia, I could understand why she would be so powerfully attracted to the Temple, but Nu-nah, who had never entered the Holy Sanctuary except for those sacred Rites that are administered to all who are supposed to be bordering on the land of the spiritual world; only those two nights, to his knowledge, had she ever been in the Sacred Sanctuary; there was something in those ceremonies that he had not as yet understood; there must have been some mystical, magical power employed to restore the frail, feeble, unconscious Nu-nah to life and health and, to him."

He thought and reasoned until his brain was on fire, and still no solution of the mystery was presented to his understanding.

"Well," he at last exclaimed, so loud that he startled

himself, "I will have to accept it as a mystery and patiently wait time's own pleasure for the explanation."

He began to prepare for retiring, but he could not calm himself — a restlessness took possession of him that he could not quell; he walked the floor, tried to read, and resorted to many ways to restore his tranquillity, but all in vain.

"I must see my Nu-nah once more before I can sleep," and, hurriedly readjusting the clothing he had removed, he repaired to the Princess' private room. A gentle knock brought the attendant to the door.

"Is the Princess quiet and sleeping," he inquired in a whisper.

"No," answered the servant. "She is awake and feeling well, and just now remarked, that if she thought you were not sleeping she would have you called for she had something she wished to tell you."

His presence was at once made known to the Princess, and, with a low cry of delight, she called him to her side. A signal sent the attendant from the room, when the Princess began, "My Rathunor, my beloved husband, I am so glad you came. I have something to tell you that I might forget before morning. Tonight, when we came within the sound of the music in the Temple, I felt as if I left my body and you, and by some unknown power was drawn into the Sacred Sanctuary. I saw the High Priest, the lovely Mother Priestess, the Vestals, the choir and musicians, all earnestly engaged in some holy ceremony. The music, the heavenly spiritual influence of the atmosphere, the exquisite fragrance of incense and perfumes, with the purity reflected by the Vestal attendants, so enraptured and enthralled me that the thought that I would ever have to leave its sacred boundaries caused me to lose consciousness and, when I awoke, you were bending over me."

Seeing a strange look in Rathunor's eyes and interpreting it to mean jealousy, she continued, "but that was not all, my Rathunor; you were there, too, for awhile. I tried to keep you, but could not — something drew you away from *me* and I, for an instant, suffered the same pangs that are torturing your heart now. I thought you would rather go than stay, and a feeling of jealousy entered my heart, but the strange fascination of the place was more to me at that instant than you, my Rathunor, so I longed to stay but could not. I have been trying to think what it all means. You must help me for already I feel the memory of the event passing away."

She ceased speaking, and in a few moments was fast asleep. The Prince kissed the hand he held, then gently laid it by her side and quietly left the room fully conscious that the mystery had been partially revealed, and that now the Princess would sleep for the rest of the night. After returning to his rooms he again flung himself into an easy chair determined to seriously think and arrive, that night, at some immediate steps to take his Nu-nah from the excitement she had been subjected to for so long, so that a recurrence of the sad event might not be repeated. Before another Sun arose the Prince had decided upon his future course. "I will take Nu-nah away, ostensibly on a long tour of the country for pleasure. Aye, for pleasure, but not the kind we have submitted to since our marriage."

The next morning, as soon as the Princess could see him, he requested her presence at once. He met her at the door and with a loving inquiry as to her health, led her to an easy chair beside the open window where the rays of the morning Sun could fall upon her as they penetrated the delicate lace which hung at the window. Drawing a chair to her side he began to unfold his plans, at the same time watching every motion and expression of the face to see what effect they would have upon her. She did not betray her thoughts until he said his object was not so much for travel as to retire to some quiet, pleasant nook, where they could be excluded from the world, and those they knew, for awhile, and instead of spending their time in the superficial pleasures of the world they could enjoy each other's society and learn something about the invisible mysteries that surrounded them.

When the motives of his plans were mentioned a perceptible change flashed across her countenance and a light appeared in her eyes that he had not seen for some time and, by the time he had finished, her whole face was beaming with an inward delight, that urged the Prince to further reveal the plans that he had laid during his midnight reasonings. The Princess raised not a single exception to his schemes but, on the contrary, entered into them with a zest that surprised even the Prince.

"O, to be alone, Rathunor, where we could think and study that which we choose has been the longing of my very soul these many weeks; can not we go at once, today if possible." She felt she could not wait the necessary time for the preparations to be made.

There was a duty toward their friends that must be fulfilled. The devoted attentions that had been showered upon them for so long must not be ignored. So, it was decided to give a farewell reception, before taking their departure for an indefinite stay in strange lands.

Accordingly invitations were issued to a grand state occasion, when the Prince and Princess would bid their friends and associates Farewell. Ah! farewell. Little did those who were of that brilliant assembly dream, as they clasped the hands of the Princess and Prince in cordial and sincere good-by, that it was indeed a Farewell to all. Neither did they conceive for a moment what those Farewells meant to the Princess and Prince. It was hard for them to conceal their happiness as every minute of time brought their departure nearer, and what their guests took for the happiness of their presence, was really induced by the thoughts of the future.

They were soon off and we can only follow them in thought for a time. Let those thoughts be kind, for, knowing thoughts are potent, send them out lovingly toward the awakening mind of Princess Nu-nah.

# CHAPTER XII.

## THE RETURN TO A NEW LIFE.

Several years have elapsed since we bade our Prince and Princess farewell. Only at long intervals had they communicated with their friends. The outer world had almost forgotten them, but not so with the Hierophant and the Priestess of the Temple. Daily, had their prayers gone in behalf of their souls' welfare. Although not in communication with them in body they were in spirit, and from this source they knew all was well. The High Priest, in his astral visits, could see the growing power of the soul over the slowly-evolving brain of the Princess, and with the electric soul-force, the great nourisher and renewer of life, though unconscious to him, the rounding out was fast nearing completion of the soul's mastery over the brain and body of Nu-nah.

They had settled in distant lands, near a little country village that lay just at the foot of the mountains. It was made up of the simple peasantry, where life was free from cant, suspicions, criticism and morbid curiosity. Here they could live and follow the bent of their minds, undisturbed and unobserved if they so wished. They kept their identity unknown yet the villagers knew from the Princess' delicate beauty of form and features she belonged to some noble family and station in life, but her kind, thoughtful bearing towards them won their love and esteem at once, and equally did they esteem the Prince for he was ever lavish with his money and attention to those who appealed to him for assistance. The mountains soon became their favorite resort. Long walks were taken daily, and rests made in the quiet nooks on the mountain side. One place particularly, became a very dear retreat to them, for never did they stop there but that some inspirations were born. It was here that Nu-nah took her first lesson from Rathunor; it was in this sacred spot that Rathunor gently but cautiously revealed to her the Initiatory Rites of the Temple that had been performed over her unconscious body. This excited an intense curiosity, if not deep interest, in Nu-nah's mind. She began to question and think and, as she thought, there came a vague, glimmering memory of the past, and when Rathunor would inquire the cause of her almost unconscious moods, she would raise her hand to silence his voice, and whisper, "I am dreaming — O, something so grand, so solemn, so sacred haunts my mind; just wait and it will all come by and by," then her dark eyes seemed to grow larger and larger and to burn with a concentrated fire.

The Prince's delight knew no bounds as these expressions led him to believe they sprang from deep desires and interests, so the time seemed to shorten for the day to come when their whole time and attention would be turned to the study of Nature's mysteries and the secrets of life be revealed to them, thus satisfying that inward longing for the realities of life. Also, he knew, the new love that had been born in Nu-nah's heart for him was more than that love that the external only can know. Its depths he could not fathom nor its source pursue, so he was content to wait that promised time, predicted by the Astrologer, that Nu-nah would lead, guide and teach him these spiritual truths and reveal to his already awakening soul the laws of the spirit.

Now, a new joy was revealed to the Prince when the Princess made him aware that a new soul had been entrusted to their tender care and keeping. The thoughts of maternity filled her heart with bliss. Blessed privilege, to bring to this plane of existence a soul awaiting incarnation in human form, to live, grow and experience on this planet the last grand objective existence that the soul can know. What care, what pleasure would she take in training that little soul to know its God and the mysteries of life and in maturity stand forth to teach mankind Wisdom and Truth.

The pleasure in preparing for its advent made days pass as minutes. Time, borne on the wings of love, passed quickly. Her soul had gained that control over the mind that it was full with pure, holy and spiritual thoughts. Her mind could not get beyond her husband and the young soul that had been transmitted to her keeping. The divine joy of love was singing in her soul. Rathunor left her alone in her happiness, knowing that in her condition any great effort on his part to draw her mind — thoughts into new channels might lead to dire results.

At last the Natalday arrived. The magnetic, as well as the physical, period of gestation being completed, to them a son was born. Never was there a human soul greeted with greater love and welcome than this one. Not only was it the offspring of the physical union, but that of the souls. Welcome, thrice welcome, to the children born of such love. The physical condition of the Princess was very critical for several days. The Prince's grief and anxiety was almost unbearable; neither sleep nor food took a moment of his time during her severe illness, and often did he think that again Nu-nah's soul would take its flight and wend its way to the realms above.

The eighth day after confinement was one of stupor and unconsciousness. Not a moment passed unheeded. It was near midnight when, the attendants having retired for a short rest, and Rathunor sat alone by her bedside, her eyes suddenly opened and bent their gaze upon him. Beautiful, calm, divine Nu-nah, her wonderful eyes shone with a surprising brilliancy and they were so riveted upon him that he dare not move, much less speak. The minutes that intervened between her waking and speaking seemed as an eternity to Rathunor.

"My darling husband, are you beside me — are you where I can speak to you, and are we alone?"

Only by a gentle pressure of the hand could he respond, and, gently laying his right hand upon her brow, he assured her by this act of his presence. She began speaking — her voice was low, yet clear and distinct, "My Rathunor, my true-soul companion, I have returned with the knowledge I now impart to you. While you so patiently and tenderly watched beside my frail and almost lifeless body, my soul was away gaining knowledge and experience in the soul-world. There I learned who I am and my relation to you. Do you know, O my Rathunor, that our souls sustain that divine relation to each other that makes us immortal, because of being complete? The whole, the two rays of the Divine Ego, are joined and blended as one in our union. Can you hear me further?"

The agitation of his grief began to assuage and he could now listen calmly and without emotion to her words.

"Yes, go on. What you have already said has been indelibly burned upon my mind and soul. Let me hear all you have to impart."

"Know you that this body was Nu-nah's and this soul that of Sarthia's?"

It was here that only by a mighty effort of his will was he able to keep in abeyance the emotions of his heart, but the superior and God-like power of an invisible Presence sustained him. The Princess took no heed of his silence and continued her revelations.

"Do you know that on the night of the full Moon, the solemn and sacred Rites performed over the unconscious bodies of Sarthia and Nu-nah in the Sacred Sanctuary of the Temple of Isis, our souls were transferred by the magical power of the High Priest and the invisible assistants? Nu-nah's soul was polarized in Sarthia's physical temple and that of Sarthia's in this of mine. Both were prostrated, even to dissolution by the malefic influence of planetary arcs, and this method was resorted to, that both our lives might be spared to round out our necessary physical existence while yet in these bodies, and also for your sake was this undertaken by our Holy Father that you might have that love which you so much craved and the longings of your soul might be satisfied with the knowledge it thirsted for. This will explain to you the great change observed at times in your Nu-nah, and the unnatural, dreamy moods that possessed me sometimes. The brain was slow to respond to the wonderfully developed soul of Sarthia and it was at those times that the soul gained the supremacy, that the greatest change would manifest. You now have the true devoted love of your soul companion and the lovely form of Nu-nah for your wife. My Rathunor, are you satisfied? If a pang of disappointment cross your heart, our darling child here may blot that out as he grows and learns our mystic lore and become also a soul companion of his fathers in climbing the ladder to higher wisdom and spheres than ours."

The Prince could not speak. He sank on his knees

beside the bed and buried his face in her bosom. Here silence was more profound and spoke deeper wisdom and contentment than ever words could do; how long he remained in this humble attitude and poured forth his gratefulness in prayer he knew not; but when he arose the Princess was sleeping quietly, the breathing, though feeble, was deeper and more even. He gently crossed her hands upon her bosom, adjusted the clothing carefully and left her side, full of a new hope he had had for many days. Life again appeared in all its glory, not a shadow appeared upon its horizon; weariness and anxiety forsook him and he went about as if walking on air, but not a word escaped his lips — nor an act betrayed his new-born joy.

When the nurses returned they at once remarked the change in the Princess. They, too, became hopeful and assured the husband that his wife would soon be well. The Princess recovered rapidly, and it was not long before her gentle presence and noble influence shed its effulgence in the home as she moved about it.

As soon as Rathunor could spare the time from Nunah's side he sent the Natal hour of his first-born to the Astrologer Priest. Anxiously did he await the reading of the stars and what they indicated for his child. The calculations were made, the judgment submitted in writing, but "Shall I transmit them to the Prince and Princess, can they yet receive and philosophically accept the revelations therein made?"

He left the study-room and repaired to the apartments of the High Priest to seek advice and instructions. Then, by the exercise of his potent will, he made the necessary observations to see if it were wise to convey the knowledge of the predictions to his children, Nu-nah and Rathunor.

"Not yet will we send the reading. Our Nu-nah has

not sufficiently recovered to bear any unpleasant news."

Rathunor became impatient and thought, at times, he would write again — the letter must have been lost — but something withheld him. At last strange forebodings haunted him. He knew too well the promptness of the Astrologer Priest; there must be something that could not be revealed to Nu-nah. He thought he was strong enough to bear resignedly all that might come, but when it did come all his forebodings had not prepared him to receive it. It was only a letter — no calculations — no reading, as indicated by the stars, was in it. The letter had been dictated by the Priest and transcribed by the scribe Hermo, and read thus:

"Our darling children, Rathunor and Nu-nah, bear bravely the news I now impart to you. Your first born, the offspring of true inspiration and soul-love, can not remain with you long in the physical form. The stars deny a prolonged life, and my interior knowledge of the planetary influence, also tells me his life upon our Earth's plane will be of short duration. His already matured soul does not need much of Earth's experience to round out its objective existence, before entering the true life in the spiritual realm; there it will remain, my dear children, ever beckoning you on, and contributing to you that energy that will ever spur you to greater effort to realize while yet in the physical form Immortal Life. Tend it carefully, but when the Great Powers that Be summon its soul to go, do not try to hold it here, but add the strength of your united prayers to its flight and bid it depart to its home in the spiritual realms above. God bless and give you the strength, my children, is the prayer of your devoted Father. Amen! Amen!"

The strength of spiritual force that seemed to accompany the letter and his loving advice imparted courage to their hearts, and instead of giving way to grief, began to philosophically reason and console themselves that God's ways were wiser than man's.

Not many months did their lovely spiritual child remain with them until its soul took its flight to realms beyond, where truly it became as a beacon-light to the souls of its parents. Its departure left the Prince and Princess sad and lonely for a time and their struggle to reconciliation was great — but this was of the heart and not of the soul. Time healed the external wound and the interior vacancy was filled by study, investigation and the development to external consciousness of the knowledge within.

Again, they became restless and plans were laid to leave their happy home near the mountains, and the devoted friends they had made among the villagers who were sorry to part with them and, as memento to their honest, noble friendship, they distributed their household and personal effects among them. They revealed to no one where they were going. They disappeared as mysteriously as they came, but where? Only one place on Earth could tempt them to leave that sacred home, where such extreme joy and sorrow were known, and that was the former home of the soul of Nu-nah, The Temple of Isis. Nu-nah was to enter as an aspirant to a Priestess, and Rathunor as a Priest King.

The Return to a New Life, was hailed with joyful welcomes from all of the Attendants of the Temple. Rathunor and Nu-nah soon passed the ceremonial Rites of the Temple and none were more faithful in their efforts and studies than these new-born children — the especial care of the High Priest and the Priestess.

We leave them here, wishing them the progress, the happiness and that Divine Peace and Understanding that comes to all Perfected Souls. God be with them.